D0500673

For Billy, Veronica, and Christopher, my pillars. To those who welcomed my rants about family history and old photographs in recent years, thank you. To Emaline, my great-great-great-great grandmother, if I could've met you this is what I'd say. –KAH

Dial Books for Young Readers
An imprint of Penguin Random House LLC, New York

First published in the United States of America by Dial Books for Young Readers,
an imprint of Penguin Random House LLC, 2023

Text copyright © 2023 by Kimberly Annece Henderson

Library of Congress Cataloging-in-Publication Data is available.

Manufactured in China • ISBN 9780593529249 • 10 9 8 7 6 5 4 3 2 1 • HH

Design by Sylvia Bi • Text set in Cotford

The publisher does not have any control over and does not assume any responsibility for author or third-party websites or their content.

Ciara LeRoy is a Cincinnati-based artist who specializes in hand lettering, murals, and embroidery. She created the lettering for this book digitally and dedicates it to her mother.

DEAR YESTERYEAR

*text by and
photographs curated by* Kimberly Annece Henderson

hand lettering by Ciara LeRoy

 Dial Books for Young Readers

To my dear yesteryears
whose presence
never fades.

Stony the road,
you've walked this earth

and paved the way
I now call home.

Dearest yesteryear
tell me your life's story.

THE ONLY ORIGINAL

University Singers of New Orleans

The depths of my imagination
stare in awe of all your glory.

I wonder, yesteryears,
how was your time spent?

Did you find a special
someone,
and love them to your
heart's content?

Tell me more, dear yesteryear.
Were you cradled by
the pages of a good book?

Or was it
time well spent,
at home?

I can see you as a team player,
in a league of your own.

I imagine you
taking an afternoon stroll to
visit with friends on some grassy knoll,
just beyond the town square.

Or perhaps you prefer not
to be disturbed underneath
your lace-trimmed parasol.

And, while I'm at it, dearest yesteryear, you sure dress to impress. You're "sharper than a tack," wearing your Sunday best.

I know it took some time and
effort to get dressed up so nice.

And how about the places you
visited to get your look just right.

Was it a trip to Tony's barber shop
for a fresh cut, or fade, or shave?

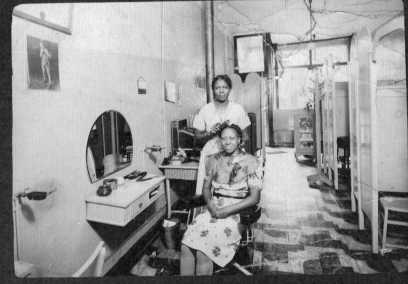

Or maybe it was Ms. Alberta's beauty parlor,
for a crimp, or curl, or finger waves?

And what about you,
little yesteryear?

Holding fast
to your mother's
embrace.

Grandpa's old-timey stories?

And mind your manners whe—

—n parents needed a brea—

Dearest yesteryear,
do you recall becoming
a man?

Were you introduced to responsibility
before your childhood had its chance?

However it happened,
dear yesteryear,
did you make it to your
dreams?

Did you write your own story?
Did you sail the seven seas?

As I reminisce,
dear yesteryear, would
you hold my hand?

And guide me by the light of your eye,
that I may better understand.

What exactly does it mean to keep your head held high?

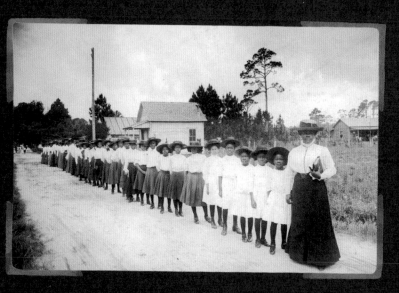

To walk and not grow weary.

To climb a mountain high.

What could it be, dear yesteryear,
that's kept you all this long?

To sleep with
one eye open,

And still sing
your siren song.

I may never feel the weight
of your words.

Or witness your smile
grow wide.

Shall nevermore subside.

So to my dearest yesteryears,
I know I'm not alone.

I'll walk within your shadow,
Until memory calls me home.

With love,
Today

Note from the Author

Trees have roots, and we each come from a long line of people who play a role in our unique life story. I am a writer, curator, and historical researcher based in New York City and have spent years researching the roots of my own family tree.

My mother's ancestors fought in the American Revolutionary War of 1776, and later formed the "Little Texas Community" in the piedmont of North Carolina. On government documents, they were often categorized as "mulatto" and were of African, European, and Indigenous descent. For generations, their livelihood was rooted in agriculture, and today, many "Little Texas" descendants identify as the Occaneechi Band of the Saponi Nation (www.obsn.org). Their story is featured in textbooks, newspaper articles, and locally preserved documentation. My maternal ancestors back into the 1700s include my third great-grandfather and a few of his brothers, who donated land and helped start a church in the name of their father, Samuel (my fourth great-grandfather). Many of my relatives served as church officials of the still active congregation, and are buried in the church's cemetery. In 2019, I journeyed to this ancestral church home and attended service during their centennial anniversary celebration, an experience that brought years of my research to life.

In the neighboring state of South Carolina, my father's ancestors experienced a radically different reality as enslaved laborers on plantations. Much of their traceable story begins after emancipation, when they migrated and settled in the piedmont of North Carolina. The unrelenting hard work of my paternal great-grandfather Jasper laid the foundation for generations of my family. My father's people were churchfolk, too. As a child, I often attended weddings, Vacation Bible School, and all kinds of functions in my father's hometown, at the very church my great-grandfather founded; without the slightest clue of his legacy there.

Though these narratives are drastically different, the one thing both of my lineages have in common is religion. My ancestors were churchgoing, Bible-thumping, fan-waving saints, with roots that run deep in the Carolinas. They worked hard, carved out a life for themselves, and created legacies that have informed many generations. The rich history of my ancestors' lives sparked my obsession with unearthing a representational visual history. I started an archival photograph project on Instagram entitled Emaline and Them (@emalineandthem), inspired by my paternal great-great-great-great-grandmother Emaline. On paper, she is among countless Black Americans who seemingly disappear into the anonymity of enslavement prior to the 1870s.

Much of what I do hinges on the ability to recall the past through photographic documentation. While most of the subjects in portraits from this era are unknown, I like to think that when I gaze upon their likeness–however long ago the portrait might've been taken–I am having a conversation with these ancestors. I see them, I hear them, and I listen to the layered stories behind their eyes, in their clothing, and how these visual cues work together to tell their story.

Each of the photographs I selected for this book spoke to me in some coded language that perhaps only the memories of my soul can fully translate. As if my own life experiences are echoed in the familiarities of what I see. It's the timelessness of smiling faces, posing for a family portrait against the backdrop of a canyon vacation as seen on page 3. It's the age-old camaraderie fueling generations of barber shops or beauty parlors, where talk of news headlines and local gossip has the power to unite complete strangers, as hot combs and clippers are put to expert use depicted in the portraits on page 14. It's the glow in the eyes of the soldiers on page 28; they were serving overseas and probably unsure of their fate, yet hopeful perhaps, after clinging to handwritten letters from loved ones.

Until I began investigating, I was unfamiliar with the scope of resources, collections, and archives that exist to preserve the breadth of the Black American experience throughout history. The images in this project were digitally sourced from historical societies, academic libraries, government databases, and other archival collections accessible online. If you would like to see similar photographs and explore related collections, visit the source websites or institutions, which are all credited on the following pages. If you're interested in researching your genealogy, creating a digital family tree and talking with your eldest relatives is a great way to start learning more about your family's history.

While I look toward the endless possibilities of our futures, I feel obligated to emphasize and acknowledge those in our everyday past. Their work laid the foundations upon which we continue to build. Dear Yesteryear is my prayer of gratitude to those individuals who've walked this path before.

"Woman standing next to a seated man against a painted backdrop." c. 1865. Stephan Loewentheil Photograph Collection. Division of Rare and Manuscript Collections, Cornell University Library. Collection number #8043.

"William Headly, escaped slave from plantation near Raleigh, North Carolina." c. 1862–1865. Carte de visite photographs from the Gladstone Collection of African Americans. Retrieved from the Library of Congress. Call number/Physical location: LOT 14022, no. 169 [P&P].

"Family on Vacation at Seven Falls in South Cheyenne Canyon, near Colorado Springs, Colorado, 1911." From the Collections of The Henry Ford. Object ID: 95.162.1

"Portrait of a woman in rocking chair." Goff, Orlando Scott, 1843–1916. Collection of the Smithsonian National Museum of African American History and Culture. Object number: 2016.5.2.42

"THE ONLY ORIGINAL University Singers of New Orleans." Collection of the Smithsonian National Museum of African American History and Culture. Object Number: 2011.155.69

"Unidentified young African American soldier in Union uniform with American flag." Liljenquist Family Collection of Civil War Photographs. Retrieved from the Library of Congress. Call Number: AMB/TIN no. 3263 [P&P]

"Full-length portrait; young man in frogged band uniform holding cornet." c. 1890. Weldon Johnson Memorial Collection in the Yale Collection of American Literature, Beinecke Rare Book and Manuscript Library. Call number: JWJ MSS 540.

"Untitled (Portrait of a Couple)." c. 1898. Nottingham Studio, Macon, Missouri. Museum Purchase: Photography Acquisition Fund, Portland Art Museum. Accession number: 2015.121.27.

"Florida State Normal and Industrial School class of 1904 portrait—Tallahassee, Florida." [Robert William Butler, John Adams Cromartie, Arthur Rudolph Grant, Walter Carolus Smith (front row at left), Rufus Jason Hawkins, Walter Theodore Young, Rosa Belle Lee, Marguerite Guinervere Wilkins [Smith] (3rd from left, top row), Sara Grace Moore, Winifred Leone Perry, Margaret Adelle Yellowhair (2nd from right, front row).] 1904. State Archives of Florida, Florida Memory. Image number RC02520.

"Dentistry at Howard University, Washington, D.C., c. 1900." Retrieved from the Library of Congress. Call Number/Physical Location: LOT 11294 [item] [P&P]

"Portrait of two unidentified African American children." c. 1865–1870. Carte de visite photographs from the Gladstone Collection of African Americans. Retrieved from the Library of Congress. Call Number: LOT 14022, no. 69 [P&P]

"African American man giving piano lesson to young African American woman." c. 1900. Du Bois albums of photographs of African Americans in Georgia exhibited at the Paris Exposition Universelle in 1900. Retrieved from the Library of Congress. Call Number: LOT 11930, no. 363 [P&P]

"Minneapolis Colored Keystones." [Names and positions are annotated on mat and identified as follows. Back row, left to right: Fred "Pop" Roberts (2nd Base), Dick "Noisy" Wallace (Right Field), Eugene "Cherry" Barton (Left Field), Charles Jessup (Pitcher), "Topeka" Jack Johnson (1st Base), Bobby Marshall (Captain, Utility), George Hopkins(Center Field), Bill Binga (3rd Base). Middle row, left to right: Walter Ball (Pitcher), Edward "Kidd" "K.F" Mitchell (Pres. Manager/Owner), Mamie Lacey Mitchell, Eddie Davis (Secretary), Andrew Campbell (Catcher). Front row, left to right: Graham (Pitcher), Arthur Irwin (Shortstop).] c. 1908. Minnesota Historical Society. Locator number: GV3.11 h5

"Young adults on grass." c. 1900. International Center of Photography, Gift of Daniel Cowin, 1990. Accession number: 762.1990.

"Full-length formal portrait of lady seated with elaborate gown, parasol in right hand and wearing large feathered hat. Photographic postcard." c. 1905. Randolph Linsly Simpson, African-American Collection. James Weldon Johnson Memorial Collection in the Yale Collection of American Literature, Beinecke Rare Book and Manuscript Library. Call number: JWJ MSS 54

"P.G. Lanvery's Band and Vaudeville Co., Season 1901. . ." Randolph Linsly Simpson, African-American Collection. James Weldon Johnson Memorial Collection in the Yale Collection of American Literature, Beinecke Rare Book and Manuscript Library. Call number JWJ MSS 54

"African American Couple." c. 1890s Missouri State Archives, African American Portrait Collection donated by Missouri State Museum Identifier number: MS339_0091.tif 00.1991.020.0025

"African-Americans In Barbershop." c. 1912 Johns Hopkins University Sheridan Libraries. Identifier number: MS.0583

"Beautician and Customer." c. 1940. International Center of Photography, Gift of Daniel Cowin, 1990. Accession No. 1277.1990

"Untitled (Portrait of a Young Girl)." c. 1900. Sandberg & Allen Studio, Omaha, Nebraska. Museum Purchase: Photography Acquisition Fund. Portland Art Museum. Accession number: 2015.121.34

"Carte-de-visite of a woman with a young boy" c. 1865. Collection of the Smithsonian National Museum of African American History and Culture, Gift of Linda and Artis Cason. Object number 2011.30.2

"Portrait of Alex Johnson Family." c. 1913 Joseph Judd Pennell Photographs Collection (1888–1923). University of Kansas Digital Collections. Call number RH PH Pennell : print 2645 : box 56 : Pennell number 1512H

"Group portrait, family of five, Cased tintype, half plate." c. 1875. Randolph Linsly Simpson African-American Collection. James Weldon Johnson Memorial Collection in the Yale Collection of American Literature, Beinecke Rare Book and Manuscript Library. Call number JWJ MSS 54

"Portrait of Mrs. Francis Pierce Boy." Joseph Judd Pennell Photographs Collection (18881923). University of Kansas Digital Collections. Call number RH PH Pennell : print 2960.1 : box 65 : Pennell number 1431I

"Ambrotype of an unidentified woman and child." c. 1860. Collection of the Smithsonian National Museum of African American History and Culture, Gift from the Liljenquist Family Collection. Object number 2011.51.11

"Hon. Josiah Thomas Walls of Florida." c. 1860–1875. Brady-Handy photograph collection. Retrieved from the Library of Congress. Call Number: LC-BH83-1815 [P&P]

"Two young African American women, probably somewhere in Virginia." c. 1910. Retrieved from the Library of Congress, Reproduction Number LC-USZ62-46762

"Two Men on the Deck of the Wanderer." c. 1905–1924. New Bedford Whaling Museum. Call number: 1991.50.2.1.

"African American Women: Seven women pose together holding hands." African American Portrait Collection donated by Missouri State Museum. Missouri State Archives. Identifier MS339_0129.tif 00.1991.020.0063

"African American Couple." African American Portrait Collection donated by Missouri State Museum. Missouri State Archives. Identifier MS339_0127.tif 00.1991.020.0061

"Young African American woman posted standing with umbrella, mutton sleeved jacket, and hat with feathers." Missouri State Archives African American Portrait Collection donated by Missouri State Museum. Identifier MS339_0001.tif T00.2008.008.0003ddd

"Portrait of Marie Watson Holding Umbrella." c. 1902. Joseph Judd Pennell Photographs Collection (1888–1923). University of Kansas Digital Collections. Call number RH PH Pennell : print 904 : box 23 : Pennell number 1192D

"Two brothers in arms." c. 1860–1870. William A. Gladstone collection of African American photographs Ambrotype/Tintype filing series. Retrieved from the Library of Congress. Call Number AMB/TIN no. 1327 [P&P]

"Mary McLeod Bethune with a line of girls from the school." c. 1911. State Archives of Florida, Florida Memory. Collection number: M95-2, Box 2

"Roger Williams University—Nashville, Tenn.—Normal class." c. 1899. Retrieved from the Library of Congress. Call number LOT 11307 [item] [P&P]

"Portrait of Anna Lovett Latham's Mother, 1901." Bullard, William, courtesy of Frank Morrill, Clark University and the Worcester Art Museum. Portrait of Anna Lovett Latham's Mother, 1901

"African-American Man On Horse." c. 1920. Johns Hopkins University Sheridan Libraries. Identifier MS.0583

"Tintype photograph of a man identified as James Turner, with two women." c. 1873. Collection of the Smithsonian National Museum of African American History and Culture. Object Number 2011.57.16.1

"Photographic postcard of soldiers in World War One at Verdun." c. 1918 [Oscar Calmeise (far right) and five other unidentified soldiers during World War One.] Collection of the Smithsonian National Museum of African American History and Culture, Gift of the Greer-Calmeise Family of Cincinnati, Ohio. Object number: 2019.18.11

"Cabinet Card of Young Woman Photographed by N. C. Shorey, of Toronto." c.1890. Rick Bell Family Fonds, Brock University.

"Photograph of Rev. and Mrs. Wright and Family signed to Mrs. Mary Bell." Rick Bell Family Fonds, Brock University

"Full-length double portrait; seated man wearing three piece suit; child in straw hat and light dress standing left." c. 1885. Randolph Linsly Simpson African-American Collection. James Weldon Johnson Memorial Collection in the Yale Collection of American Literature, Beinecke Rare Book and Manuscript Library. Call number JWJ MSS 54

"A portrait of a young Black woman in a light coloured dress." c. 1860. Rick Bell Family fonds, RG 63, Brock University Archives